Wonder Bear

by Tao Nyeu

templar publishing

For my parents

A TEMPLAR BOOK

First published in the UK in 2009 by Templar Publishing,
an imprint of The Templar Company plc,
The Granary, North Street, Dorking, Surrey, RH4 IDN, UK
www.templarco.co.uk

Originally published in the United States in 2008 by Dial Books for Young Readers,
a division of Penguin Young Readers Group,
345 Hudson Street, New York, New York 10014, U.S.A.
www.penguin.com/youngreaders

The artwork was silkscreened using water-based ink.

First edition

ISBN 978-1-84011-769-1

Manufactured in China on acid-free paper

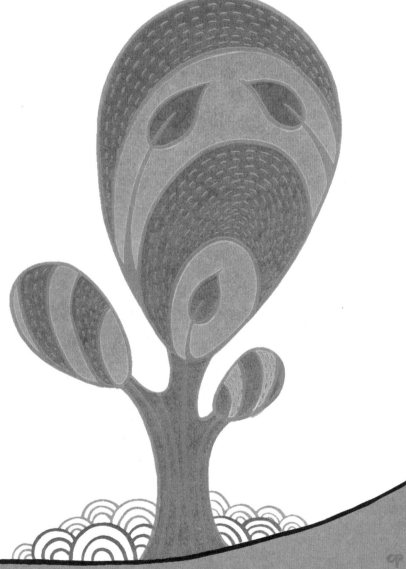
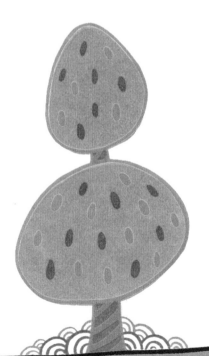

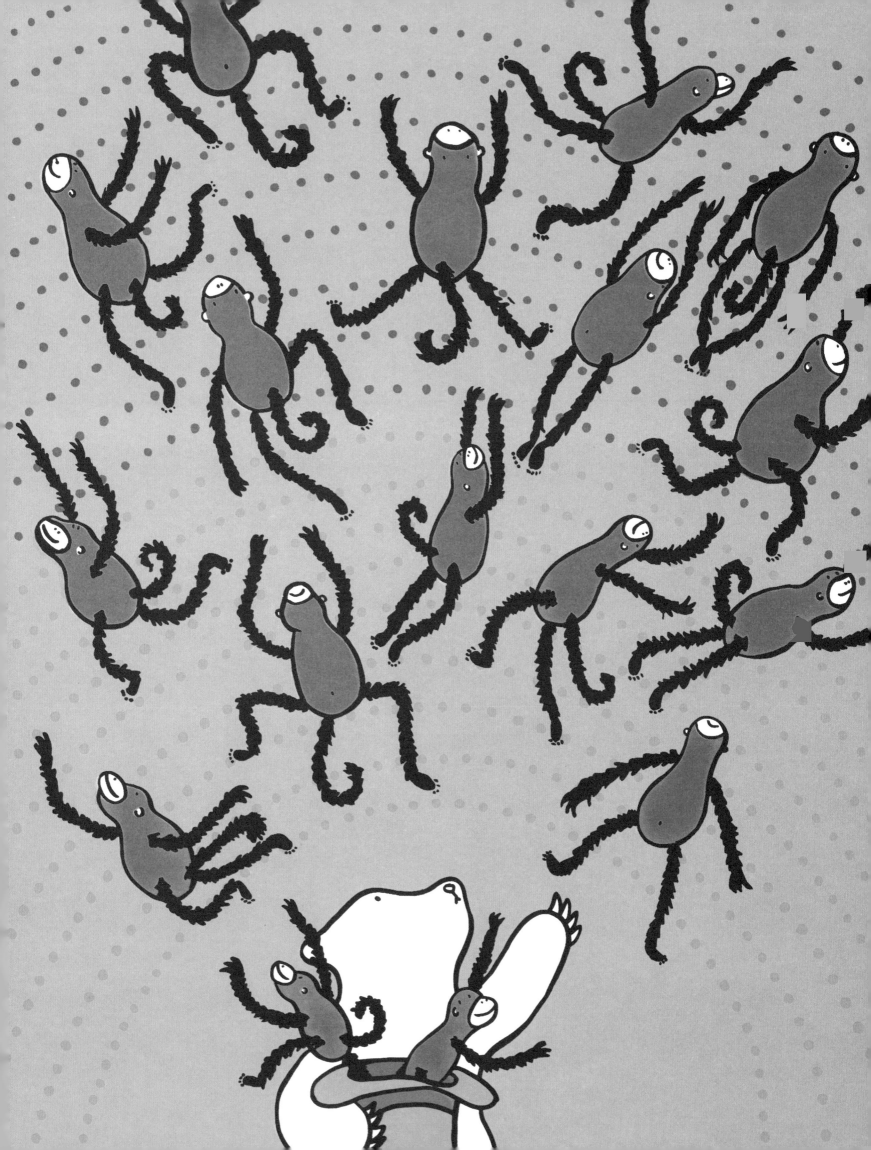